THE ADVENTURES OF MR. QUIGGLEY:

The Male Beta

MARGARETHA BROWN

PAGE PUBLISHING, INC.
New York, NY

First originally published by Page Publishing, Inc. 2016

ISBN 978-1-68348-914-6 (Paperback)
ISBN 978-1-68348-915-3 (Digital)

Printed in the United States of America

Mr. Quiggley lived in the pet shop, where he was born. His house was made of glass, clean and comfy, filled with very special water. The bottom was covered with shiny stones; dark blue, bright red, and grass green. Sometimes, he saw his reflection in the other glasshouses next to him; as a matter of fact, they seemed to be everywhere.

Mr. Quiggley was a bright red color with hues of dark blue and violet on his feathery tail. The colors even became darker when he was mad or scared. Even though he saw all the other fish around him, he got very lonely. There was no one to talk to or love him.

4

One day, a family came into the pet shop and stopped in front of his glasshouse. There were smiles on their faces, and the little boy tapped on his house. The next moment, the pet shop owner picked up Mr. Quiggley with his glasshouse and placed him into the boy's hands.

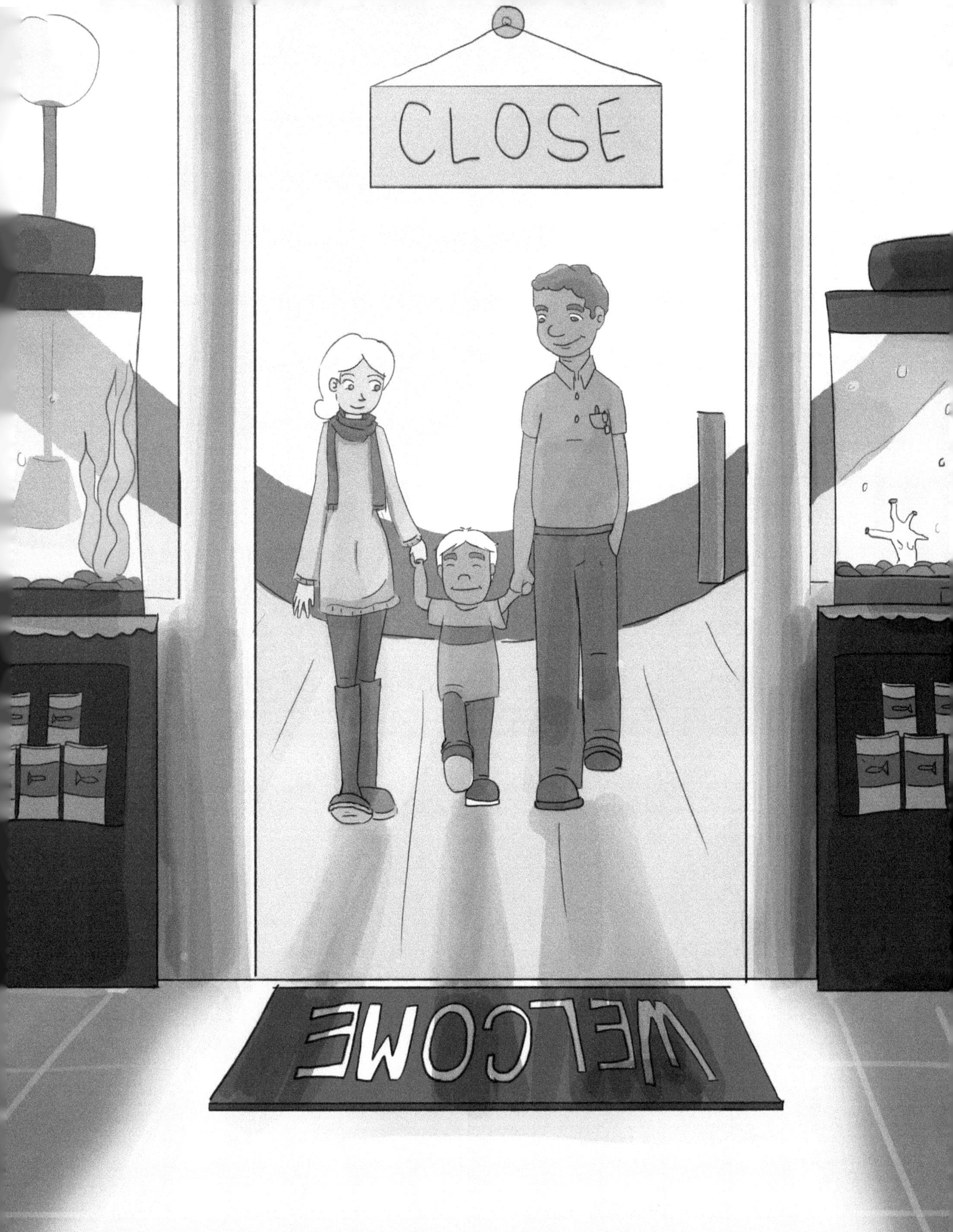
CLOSE
WELCOME

They took him outside. He had never been out of the pet shop and was becoming afraid. Oh, how strange! he thought, as the sun warmed his skin. The light was also brighter than he had seen, and that breeze, was it the wind?

Mr. Quiggley's house began to shake, and there were waves all around him. He was being swished back and forth and beginning to get really sick; but suddenly, the waves stopped. A door opened, and he saw four wheels. Could that be a car? He questioned. It was rather pleasant.

A door opened, and he was placed in a special spot where the sun shined upon him. There were no other glasshouses to be seen. He felt lonely and hungry. Then he heard different voices. The little boy picked up his glasshouse taking him to the biggest room he had ever seen.

Mr. Quiggley became really scared someone was trying to get him out of his house with a net. OH NO! Here it comes. SPLASH! SPLASH! Into a new glasshouse he went. He was hoping that it was filled with that "special water" from the pet shop. Looking around, he was surprised.

There on the bottom among the beautifully colored stones were seashells. The ones that his parents told him were only found in the sea. He swam and swam so happily on top of them, under them, and around them. Oh my goodness! What was this? He bumped into something he had never seen before. A SNAIL! "HELLO, HELLO." Mr. Snail was not speaking, but hiding under the colored rocks. Mr. Quiggley, trying to get his attention, nudged him with his nose in order to give him a gentle tickle. Mr. Snail still didn't move or pay him any attention. He just began to make his way onto the side of the glasshouse. Quiggley could only dance in the water. His parents told him never to swim upside down, people didn't like that; they would put you in many unlikely places. All this excitement made Quiggley really hungry. Not one of the smiling faces took notice. The man at the pet shop always had food when he was hungry. He began to blow air bubbles on the top of the water and even stuck his nose above the water. Still, nothing happened. Then he performed his most graceful dance. Mr. Snail, in the meantime, was climbing the glass stuck, once again, in one place.

The smiling faces finally came home having food in their hands. Quiggley performed his most perfect dance and showed all his brilliant colors. Food began to float on top of the water, and he couldn't wait to eat. As soon as he gulped down the food. Oh no! It's shrimp. He didn't like that kind of food. He danced in circles around, over and under the colored rocks bumping into Mr. Snail. This time hurting his nose. The snail let go of the glass and sank to the bottom resting on one of the seashells. Hopefully, the smiling faces fed him the food that he liked. Surfacing, he blew bubbles and beheld morsels of real food appears! Tomorrow will be a much better day.

Fish, as people, have feelings and want a midnight snack.

THE HOT TUB

All was quiet in the glasshouse with Mr. Snail napping, as usual, on top of one of the seashells, always keeping to himself and ignoring everyone else. Perhaps, he would be happier if the smiling faces put in another snail to live with us.

Quiggley was enjoying his day blowing bubbles on top of the water with the sun shining from the window, touching the glass rocks making them look like rare jewels. UH-OH! The house began to shake, and there was an unusual loud noise. The special water began to disappear, having to dive very deep lying close to a seashell. It was beginning to be hard to breathe. Looking up, he saw a big tongue and a black nose. It was one of those animals that he heard his parents talking about. The smiling faces called them dogs, and it was drinking his special water. It was a long time before the noise stopped. There was barely enough water to cover Quiggley's nose. Where was Snail? Still perched on top of the seashell. His ears must be plugged with wax, or he is deaf.

The family finally came into the room. Their faces weren't smiling. The dad picked up the glasshouse and Quiggley along with Snail were swishing back and forth, making both of them sick. His hand lowered to pick up both of them, placing them in a small glass cup filled with that special water. Quiggley was grateful, but something was different. His skin began to feel really warm, and his gills began to burn. This did not feel good. He began to dance faster and faster and faster. He had to get out of this hot water. Finally, he bumped against the small glass and out he jumped. He was flying just like a bird. When he quit flying, he landed on something hard and cold. No birds or special water. He tried to dance or blow bubbles, but all that came out was a gasp of air. The ground began to shake, and his body jumped up and down. The smiling faces were running to catch him. The big hands, at last, cradled him and placed him in his house and special water. Mr. Snail, missing all the excitement, was still atop the seashell. There is no place like home!

THE VACATION

The lights went on much too early finding Quiggley asleep, only his gills were moving, the rest of him making no movement in the water. Snail was hugging his favorite blue stone. This was a different day for the smiling faces; they were in a hurry with loud voices and slamming doors. All this noise put Snail in an ill mood. He left his favorite place and slowly moved up the side of the glasshouse. One of the smiling faces tapped the glass which frightened him, causing him to slide down, and hiding behind some of the seashells. Into the water came a pill, it was like fireworks.

Pretty colors exploded in the water, and it was tasty, even Snail enjoyed the treat. Then silence. The lights did not come on until morning and no smiling faces or loud noises. Snail was going around in circles, eventually making Quiggley dizzy, before climbing the side of the house and dropping to the bottom. Hugging his favorite rock and then hiding behind a seashell. Quiggley, looking for something to do, followed behind. He never saw Snail's eyes before, how strange. Then all of a sudden, the head disappeared within his shell. There was a door covering his shell. What now?

Quiggley swam around and around attempting to open the unusual covering. Suddenly, there appeared two eyes, seemly on top of a ladder. How could this be? His parents never prepared him for such an encounter. The silence was disturbed by the opening of the front door. Yeah! The smiling faces have returned. So glad that life was back to normal.

Good night, sleep tight, don't let the bedbugs bite.

ABOUT THE AUTHOR

Margaret P. Brown is an immigrant from Austria, who settled with her family in Lawton, Oklahoma in 1958. She arrived in the states without the ability to speak English.

She has a living mother, two sisters, 4 children and eleven grandchildren. After living in Wichita Falls, Texas, she now resides in Oklahoma City, Oklahoma with her husband, Bill.

Her career of 45 years in the medical field as a certified surgical tech ended in 2015 and is now retired.

CPSIA information can be obtained
at www.ICGtesting.com
Printed in the USA
BVHW020948131021
618834BV00018B/747